Cloud

Space Rocket

Moon

Space Helmet

Pole

Small Boat

Passenger Friend

Ball

Propeller

Tools

Roller Skates

Papa Bear

Martian

.Penguin is for Sarah-Jane
for pauline Em Mum Gray & Mark.
.K M & B.
My warmest thanks to Sue & to Susannah
& especially to Jennifer..
(my propeller).

Text and illustrations copyright © 1992 Rodney Rigby.
All rights reserved. Printed in Hong Kong.
First published 1992 by ABC, All Books for Children,
a division of The All Children's Company Ltd.,
33 Museum Street, London WC1A 1LD, United Kingdom.
First published in the U.S. by Hyperion Books for Children,
114 Fifth Avenue, New York, New York 10011.

FIRST EDITION
1 3 5 7 9 10 8 6 4 2

Library of Congress Cataloging-in-Publication Data
Rigby, Rodney.
Hello, this is your penguin speaking/Rodney Rigby — 1st ed.
p. cm.
Summary: With a little mechanical assistance, Penguin
succeeds in realizing his desire to fly.
ISBN 1-56282-231-4 — ISBN 1-56282-232-2 (lib. bdg.)
[1. Penguins — Fiction. 2. Flight — Fiction.] I. Title.
PZ7.R44178He 1992
[E] — dc20 91-39501
CIP
AC

The artwork for each picture is prepared using
colored pencil, watercolor, and pen and ink.
This book is set in 18-point Fournier.

Hello, This Is Your Penguin Speaking

RODNEY RIGBY

Hyperion Books for Children

Penguin was reading his favorite book. "I wish
I could fly and carry passengers like an airplane,"
he thought. " 'Welcome to Penguin Airlines,'
I'd announce, and *vroom!* take off."

Penguin knew that airplanes had big
wings. "Just like mine," he thought.
    And he saw that they had wheels for
landing and takeoff. "*Almost* like mine,"
he thought, looking at his feet.

Penguin was so excited he
started dancing and flapping.

"What are you doing, Penguin?" asked his friends.
Penguin stopped dancing and flapping. "I'm an
airplane," he answered. His friends tried not to
smile, but a few laughed behind their flippers.

And when Penguin told them about his idea,
Penguin Airlines, they all just laughed out loud.

Even though no one really believed Penguin could
fly, news traveled fast, and soon everyone was excited.
On the day of the first flight, a large crowd
gathered. "Welcome to Penguin Airlines," announced
Penguin proudly.

And he flapped
and flapped and
started to run.

"Hello!" he shouted. "This is your Penguin speaking."
"Hello," said the first passenger.
"Prepare for takeoff!"
said Penguin.

RUN!

With one more flap and a little hop and a skip,
Penguin lifted both feet off the ground.
"Wheeee!" sang Penguin and his passenger . . .

. . . and they crashed with a splashy *plop!*
"Hooray!" everyone cheered. "Me next!"

"I need more height," said Penguin, dragging the next passenger to the top of an iceberg.

"I've never flown before," said the new passenger nervously, climbing on board.

"Don't worry—I haven't either," said Penguin. "Not really."

After a count of
"1, 2, 3, JUMP!"
Penguin did just that.
"Flap!" he shouted to his
passenger, but his passenger
was too scared to move.

Plop! Penguin crashed a second time, with a bigger splash.

Everyone was very excited. "WOW!" they cheered. "Me next! Me next!"

But as he was brushing the snow off
his flippers, Penguin had a better idea.

He gathered some wood and some nails and a hammer,
a saw for cutting and a ruler for measuring, and a big
bucket of the reddest red paint, and then he set to work.

When he had finished, he tried the propeller for size. Perfect! Then he strapped on an extra fast pair of roller skates for takeoffs.

"Just like a real airplane," Penguin thought proudly.

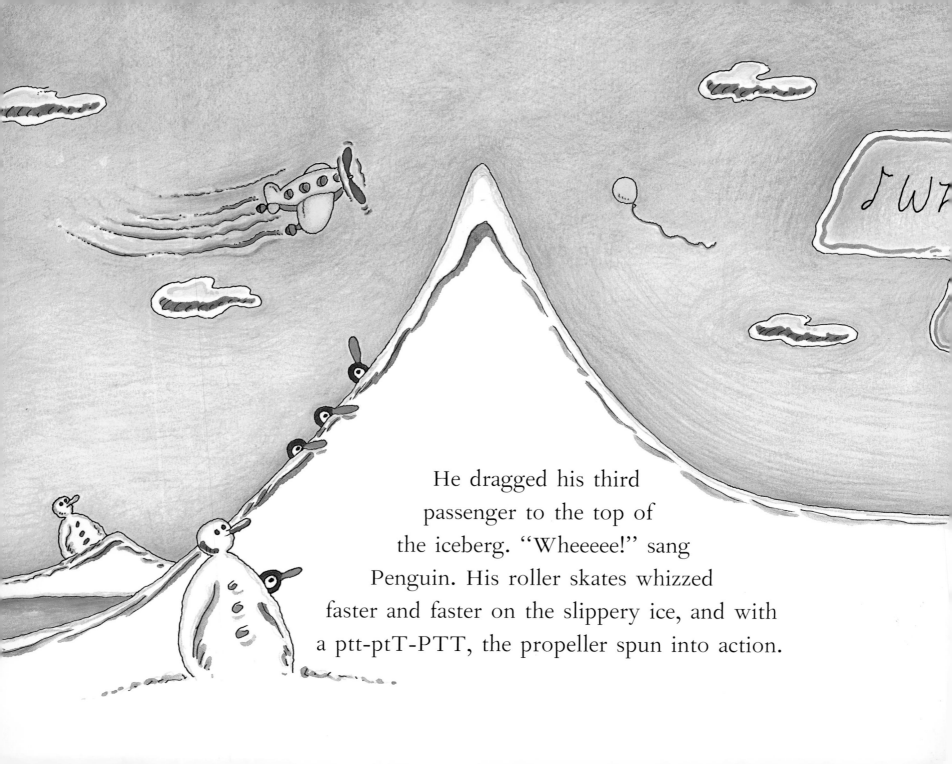

He dragged his third
passenger to the top of
the iceberg. "Wheeeee!" sang
Penguin. His roller skates whizzed
faster and faster on the slippery ice, and with
a ptt-ptT-PTT, the propeller spun into action.

Penguin lifted his head to the breeze.

"Hello!" screamed Penguin
above the noise of the whirring
propeller. "This is your Penguin
speaking." His passenger held on tightly,
and *vroom!* they leaped off.

Up they flew,
higher and higher, until
the world was below them.
"Wow!" they exclaimed. And when
the propeller stopped whirring, they came
back down to earth with a splashy PLOP!

Penguin's new idea was his best ever. "Welcome to Penguin Space Shuttle," he said to his first passenger. "This is your Penguin speaking. I hope you'll have a pleasant trip."

"Thank you," said his friend nervously.
"I've never flown before."
"Don't worry—I have," said Penguin
proudly. "Prepare for takeoff!"

Stars

Airplane

Martian Mobile

Big Boat

Sout[h]

Penguin

Snowpenguin

Balloon

chocks

Baby Bear

Red Paint &